The Missing Wheel

Mary Ann Hoffman

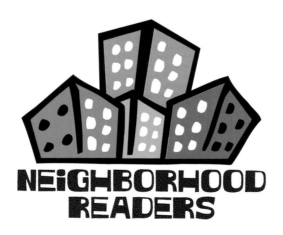

NEiGHBORHOOD READERS

Rosen Classroom Books & Materials™

New York

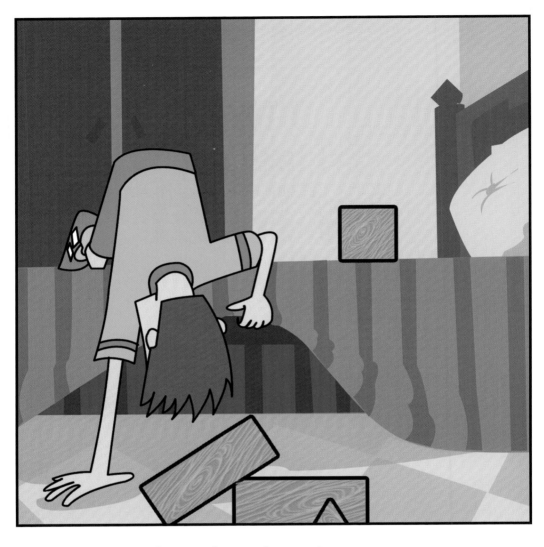

Is it under the bed?

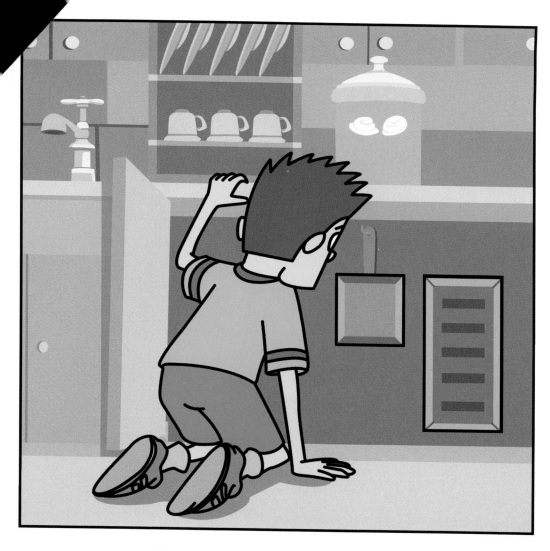

Is it in the kitchen?

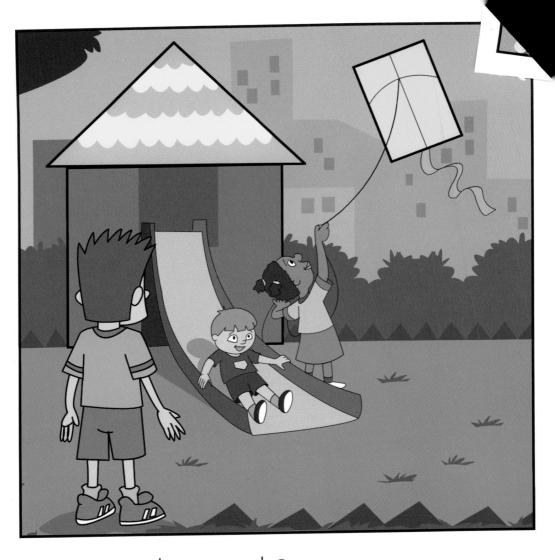

Is it in the park?

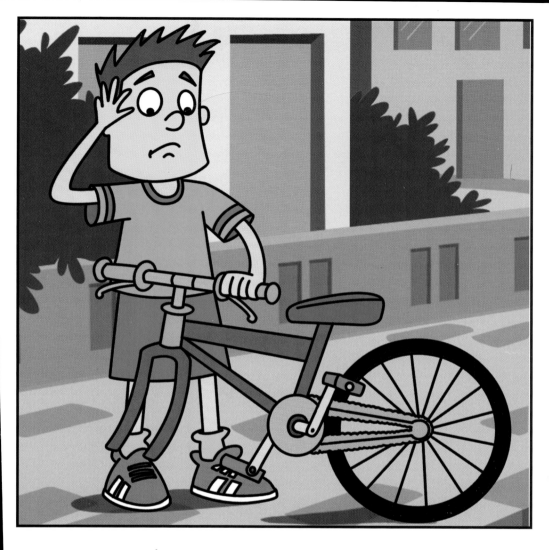

Is it in the street?

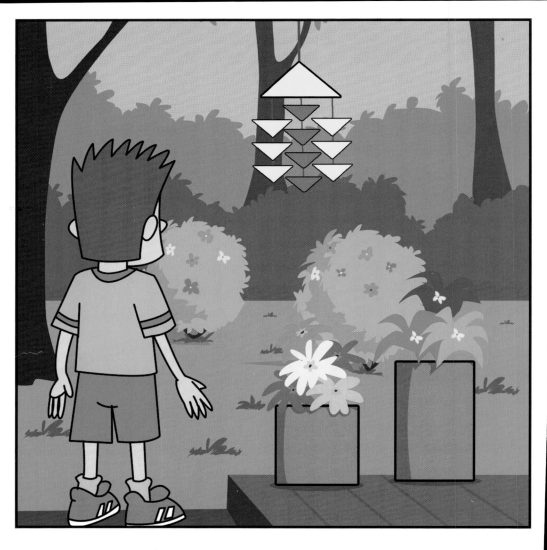

Is it in the yard?

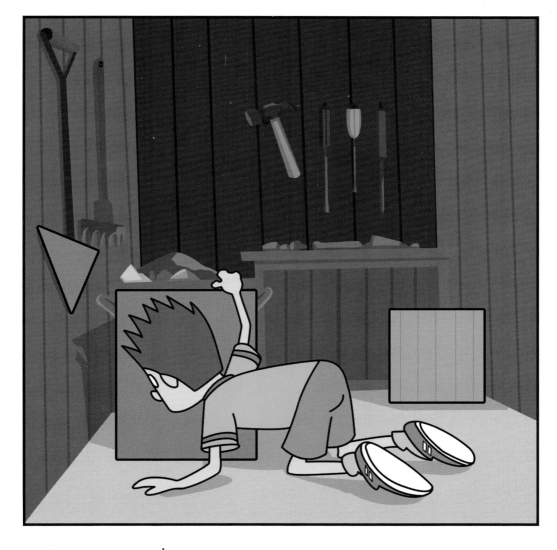

Is it in the garage?

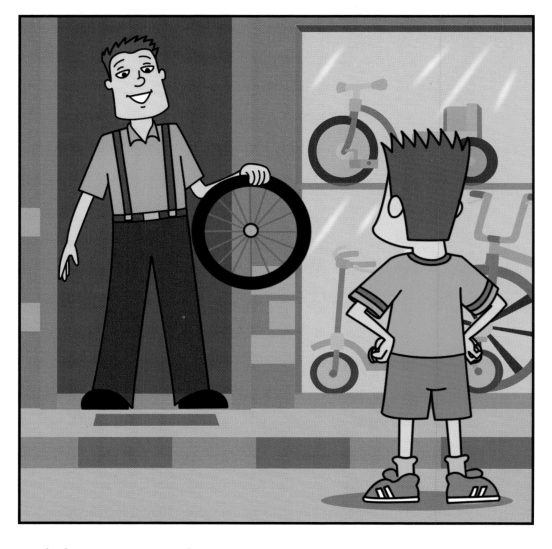

Here it is!